CATCH ME
if you can

Get to know the girls of

Catch Me
if you can

BY
THALIA KALKIPSAKIS

ILLUSTRATED BY
ASH OSWALD

SQUARE
FISH

FEIWEL AND FRIENDS
NEW YORK

SQUARE
FISH

An imprint of Macmillan Publishing Group, LLC
175 Fifth Avenue
New York, NY 10010
mackids.com

Our books may be purchased in bulk for promotional,
educational, or business use. Please contact your local
bookseller or the Macmillan Corporate and Premium Sales
Department at (800) 221-7945 ext. 5442 or by e-mail at
MacmillanSpecialMarkets@macmillan.com.

ISBN 978-1-250-12939-0 (paperback)

Library of Congress Cataloging-in-Publication Data Available

Originally published in Australia by E2,
an imprint of Hardie Grant Egmont.
Originally published in the United States by Feiwel and Friends
First U.S. edition, 2008
Square Fish reissue edition, 2017
Book designed by Ash Oswald
Square Fish logo designed by Filomena Tuosto

1   3   5   7   9   10   8   6   4   2

AR: 3.7

CHAPTER ❀ ONE

I closed my eyes and puckered up my lips. This was it—my first kiss.

I could hear my best friend Alex next to me. She was talking loudly, telling Callum and me to get ready. Two of Callum's friends were muttering and giggling.

I was breathing through my nose and could smell the pine needles at our feet.

"On your mark," Alex yelled.

I squeezed my eyes shut even tighter, wondering what my first kiss was going to feel like. Wet? Soft? Slimy and gooey?

I had kissed grown-ups on the cheek before. But I knew that was nothing like this. This was big. This was important. I was going to remember my first kiss for the rest of my life.

"Get set," Alex said.

She was almost squealing with excitement.

I started breathing faster, too. But I wasn't excited anymore. I was scared. I wasn't sure if I wanted to do this with everyone watching.

"Go!" Alex squealed.

I held my breath, puckered my lips again, and waited.

My first kiss?

Nothing happened. I could still hear Callum's friends giggling.

I opened my eyes.

Callum was standing opposite me with one foot in front of the other, like he was about to run a race. He's tall, so he was hunched over to be at my level.

He was leaning forward and frowning as if this was the most important thing in his life.

"Come on, Becky," Alex said.

She bumped me with her hip. I bumped her back. I wasn't sure what else to do. I didn't want to look at Callum.

I have known Callum for years. Our moms are friends, so I see him all the time. But we are linked in other ways, too. Last year we both gave speeches at a school concert. And now we're the only kids in our class allowed to use pens instead of pencils.

So, as Alex always says, we're a perfect match.

"Come on!" Alex said again.

"This feels dumb," Callum said quietly.

His friends started making slurpy kissing noises and wrestling with each other.

I looked down at my feet and kicked at some pine needles. When I looked up again, Callum was looking at me. I think he felt the same as I did—we didn't want to do this with everyone watching.

"Yeah, this is dumb," I said, turning around to Alex.

But I felt a little disappointed.

"Becky!" said Alex. She had her hands on her hips, like she always does when she's telling people what to do. "We've been planning this for days!"

I shrugged. "Well, it doesn't feel right."

One of Callum's friends grabbed him around the waist. So Callum dived on top of him. Soon, all three of them were rolling in the dusty pine needles, play punching and pretend kissing.

Alex looked sternly at me and raised her eyebrows.

"Why don't *you* do it, then?" I whispered to Alex.

This whole thing had started because Alex liked Mickey, one of Callum's friends.

But somehow, Alex had planned it that Callum and I had to go first.

Alex shook her head and her cheeks went pink. I giggled. I wasn't used to Alex being shy.

By now, the three boys were running among the trees, playing tag. But they didn't stray far from Alex and me.

Then, as Callum ran past, he tagged me on the arm.

"Becky's it!" he screeched as he ran away, heading for the field.

Of course, I tagged Alex in an instant, and was off after the boys before she could even get her hands off her hips.

It felt good to be running and laughing

again after thinking so much about my first kiss.

But as I caught up with the boys in the middle of the field, Alex called out from behind me.

"I've got it!" she yelled.

We all stopped running and looked at her. As she reached us, she did a dramatic leap and spread her arms out for effect.

"Kissy tag!" Alex said, as she landed.

Mickey nodded and smiled.

But Callum laughed. "Yeah, but you girls can't catch us boys!" he said.

By now I had my hands on *my* hips. "We can catch you, no problem!" I said.

We all started giggling then, and trying

to figure out the rules of kissy tag.

I smiled at Callum and he smiled back.

We still had a chance at our first kiss.

CHAPTER *TWO*

At lunchtime the next day, we all ran laughing to the pine tree area, ready to play kissy tag.

None of us really knew how to play. We couldn't work out how to tag someone with a kiss. How do you kiss when you're running?

So we all decided that if you were tagged like normal, you had to stop running and let the other person kiss you.

As I put my foot in the circle, I looked over at Callum. He was frowning a little, with his hands on his knees. But his eyes were shining.

I like it when his eyes look like that.

Alex bent down and started counting out our feet. "Eeney meeney miney mo, catch a tiger by its toe. . . ."

I had an image in my mind of Callum chasing me to a quiet spot, maybe in the back of the pine tree area.

When we were by ourselves, I would slow down. He would tag me when no one else was looking. And then . . .

I never imagined what I would do if

I was it. So when all the counting finished and I was left with my foot in the circle, I just stood there, surprised.

I was it!

I could see Alex through the trees, running towards the field. But as I turned around, I realized I had no idea where Callum was. I hadn't even seen him run off.

I started dashing between the pine trees, jumping over tree roots and checking behind the trunks. But I couldn't find Callum. In fact, I couldn't find any of my friends.

My heart was pumping fast. I ran out of the shade of the pine trees and looked across the field.

There, standing in a group on the baseball field, were Callum and his friends.

For a moment, I wasn't sure what to do. *Does Callum want me to run down and tag him on the field with everyone watching? Why is he just standing there with his friends?*

But then Callum's words from yesterday came back to me. He didn't think I could catch him. That was why he was just standing there!

In an instant, I started sprinting towards the field. I could feel my fists clenched tight and hear the dirt crunching and sliding under my feet.

I had to catch Callum.

He was tall and good at sports. But still,

I had to catch him. I had to prove him wrong.

I was over the fence and speeding across the grass before Callum even noticed I was coming. He jolted when he did see me. Then he turned around and started sprinting away.

As I dashed past his friends, they laughed and Mickey yelled out, "Go get him, Becky!"

But I didn't even look at them. All I could think of was moving my legs and pumping my arms.

All I could think of was catching Callum.

When he thought he was a safe distance away, Callum turned around and called out, "Catch me if you can!"

Then he laughed and ran backwards for a while, as if he didn't have to try very hard.

But I just kept on coming, like a train with no breaks. I didn't even waste breath on answering him or laughing.

I was going to catch that boy. . . .

CHAPTER THREE

I stayed focused and kept running.

Callum was still laughing and running backwards, but he wasn't very fast like that. The distance between us was getting smaller.

Callum must have noticed I was getting closer, because suddenly he stopped smiling. He turned around and bolted.

But the time he had wasted calling out

and running backwards meant that I was close. Now, I was right on his heels.

I kept pumping my arms and breathing in rhythm. He was fast, but I was close enough now. I just had to stay with him.

If he slowed down to jump the fence or even change direction, that's when I would have him. I was right behind him, thinking about reaching out and tagging him.

Then suddenly, Callum fell.

I was so close to him that I had to jump over him to avoid falling on top of him.

I looked down as I jumped, and saw his tall body in a strange tangle beneath me.

Then, as I landed, Callum let out a sobbing cry that seemed to echo around the field and back. It was the kind of cry that kids our age normally only let out in front of their parents—groaning and desperate and really scared.

Something was very, very wrong.

Panting, I found my balance and looked down at Callum.

"Are you OK?" I asked, even though it was clear that he wasn't.

Callum was crying really loudly. His friends ran up to us.

"What did you do?" Mickey yelled at me.

I just looked at him, stunned and scared about what was happening. But I didn't answer, it seemed like a strange question.

"He needs help!" I screamed at them.

Then I turned around and bolted for the teacher's lounge.

After that our teacher, Mrs. Tran, came over and helped Callum up. They walked slowly to the nurse's office with a bunch of kids crowded around them.

I felt sick from the running and the worry. Alex was holding my hand and asking what had happened. But I couldn't talk yet. I kept hearing Callum's cry echoing in my head.

I had never heard a boy make a sound like that before.

What had happened to him?

Callum disappeared into the nurse's office with the teacher and his friends.

Oh, no!
What happened
to Callum?

Everyone else ran off to play.

Alex and I stood outside the old door that's closest to the nurse's office.

"What happened?" Alex asked for the millionth time.

Her eyes looked big and scared.

I shook my head. "I don't know," I said. "He just fell. . . . "

For a moment, we just looked at each other. Then I pushed at the door and walked inside.

It was strange seeing the hallway so empty. Usually it's full of kids and bags and noise. Now it seemed like a place I'd never been before.

Alex was clutching my sleeve, like we

were in a horror movie or something.

We tiptoed past a couple of doors to reach the nurse's office. Lucky for us, the teacher's lounge was further down the hall.

Alex and I held hands and listened at the door.

"I've called your parents," we heard Mrs. Tran say. "We'll meet them at the hospital. I'm going to bring my car around to the front of the school. OK?"

I didn't hear Callum reply, but then the door opened and Mrs. Tran rushed out. She didn't even see Alex and me. Or if she did, she was thinking about other things.

For a while I listened at the door, but I couldn't hear anything. It didn't seem like Callum's friends were with him. Maybe they had already been sent outside.

Alex tugged at my hand like she wanted to go outside, too.

But I had to see Callum. I let go of Alex's hand, pushed at the door, and went into the nurse's office.

CHAPTER FOUR

Inside, Callum was alone on the bed. He had ice packs on his shoulder, and wet cheeks.

He lay still, as if it hurt to move.

I tried to smile, but I didn't know what to say. A flood of questions filled my mind. *What happened? Are you OK? Do you know what's wrong?* But none of them seemed like the right thing to say.

In the end, it was Callum who spoke first. I wasn't expecting him to talk, but when he did, my throat went tight.

Without moving his head, Callum said quietly, "Becky, why did you trip me?"

"I—I didn't trip you!" I said.

Then I heard the door behind me, and Mrs. Tran came in.

"Outside please, Becky," she said quickly.

So I had to go outside with Alex while Mrs. Tran took Callum to the hospital.

When Callum's mom Debbie is happy, she gets funny laugh lines around her eyes.

I like it when she looks like that. But that was the last kind of face I was expecting to see when Mom and I knocked on the door that night.

But Debbie was smiling, and she kept smiling when she looked at me, which was even more of a surprise.

My mom and Debbie had already spoken on the phone, so we knew what had happened at the hospital.

Callum had a broken collarbone. That meant he had to wear a sling for six whole weeks. It was the arm that he writes with, so he was going to have trouble writing, too. And as for basketball . . .

It was pretty bad, really. So I had no

idea why Debbie looked like she had been laughing.

"Come in, ladies," Debbie said.

Mom gave her a bunch of flowers and they went into the kitchen to find a vase.

Normally, I would have run off to find Callum, but I wasn't sure if he wanted to see me.

Plus, I didn't know what he'd said to Debbie. *Was he still saying that I tripped him? Did he tell her we'd been playing kissy tag?*

"He's in the family room, Bec," Debbie called out.

She still had those laugh lines around her eyes.

I started walking slowly up the hall.

Before I had gone far, I heard Debbie whisper something to Mom.

Then my mom let out a shriek and said, "Aren't they a little young for that?"

Then they both started laughing.

I heard Debbie say, "Our little babies are growing up!"

At least now I knew why Debbie had been laughing. Callum had told her about kissy tag!

Now I picked up my pace, frowning as I walked. I couldn't understand why Callum had told his mom about kissy tag. *Why would he do that?*

So when I got to the family room, I wasn't exactly in a happy mood.

Callum was lying on the couch, trying to play his Game Boy with one hand.

I slumped down in a chair just as I heard his game finish.

Callum threw the Game Boy onto the

floor. I don't think he could play with one hand. For a while we just sat there, saying nothing.

Then I leaned forward in the chair. "Why did you tell your mom about kissy tag?" I asked.

"Because I broke my collarbone," he said, without looking at me. "Or didn't you notice?"

"Look, I'm really sorry about that," I said.

But I was getting annoyed. I picked up the Game Boy.

"So, you're sorry you tripped me?" Callum said, moving to look at me. I could tell it hurt to move.

Why did he keep saying that?

"No," I said. "I didn't trip you, Cal."

"Not on purpose," said Callum.

He was in a pretty bad mood, and I told him so.

After that, Callum stopped talking to me. He just lay on the couch, frowning into space.

I sat in the chair, playing his Game Boy. I felt sorry for Callum—a broken collarbone was pretty bad. But I felt angry with him, too.

Why did he keep saying that I tripped him?

When it was time to go home, I didn't even say bye to Callum. I just ran out to Mom, feeling angry.

I was almost glad that I hadn't caught Callum when we played kissy tag.

CHAPTER FIVE

The next morning at school, Callum wasn't there. But other than that, nothing seemed unusual. At least, that was how the day started.

During assembly, I was up in front with the recorder group, playing "America the Beautiful." We're pretty good these days—nice and loud.

At the beginning of the year, the

principal used to set up the microphone in front of us, but now he doesn't even bother.

We ended with a really loud note that seemed to echo through the school.

But that was when everything stopped being normal.

Instead of talking about the latest field trip to the zoo, or how much garbage was lying around, the principal started talking about something else.

Along with football, where you get tackled to the ground, kissy tag was now officially banned from our school.

Of course, that was fine with me. Callum was being so mean, I didn't care about kissy tag anymore. Well, not really.

But as the principal kept talking, I started to realize that the rest of the school wasn't looking at him.

Being up front for recorder meant that I could see everyone's faces. And they were all looking at me.

The younger kids had that dumb, blank look they get. But they were definitely looking past the principal, at me.

Even the teachers were looking at me. Most of them had that "teacher frown" that they do so well. But Mrs. Tran was smiling, just like Debbie last night.

News gets around pretty fast in my school!

Even the kids in my class were giggling

or whispering and looking at me. Some of the boys were scowling like they hated me.

In fact, the only people who *weren't* looking at me were Alex and Mickey. They were looking at each other, and talking quietly. I couldn't hear what they were saying, but Alex definitely didn't look happy.

I wasn't happy either.

Why is everyone blaming me?

Callum's collarbone wasn't my fault! But everyone was blaming me.

When he finally got to the end of his lecture, the principal said, "I'm sure we won't have any more trouble with kissy tag now, will we?"

Then, in front of the whole school, he turned and looked at me.

Lunchtime was pretty bad, too. I was sitting on the steps with Alex when a bunch of little kids ran up, giggling and whispering.

"That's her there!" one of them shouted, pointing at me.

Then they all ran away, like I was going to eat them up.

Alex laughed. "You're famous now, Bec!"

But I wasn't laughing.

Then Mickey and Brad walked up, and things got serious.

"You're lucky we don't beat you up," Brad said to me.

"It was an accident, you dummy!" Alex yelled. She stood up and put her hands on her hips.

I started to think about where I would run if I needed to get away quickly. But I didn't think he really meant it.

"Well, there are accidents," Mickey said, all serious. "And there are *accidents*."

"What does that mean?" I asked.

But the boys just gave me an angry look and walked away.

"Geez!" I said, shaking my head.

This was getting silly.

"Ooooh, I *hate* Mickey," Alex said. Her mouth was tight. "He's so . . . yuck."

"You didn't think that yesterday," I said, and raised my eyebrows.

"Yeah, well," Alex said, as she sat down and picked up her sandwich. "That was before."

After that, we just sat there eating quietly. But I was thinking it all through. Alex didn't seem to like Mickey anymore.

How do you know if the person you like is

worth it? And how can you tell if he likes you?

I used to feel sure that Callum liked me—the way he used to steal my bag or my pen, like he wanted me to notice him. Or he would pull my hair like he wanted to be near me.

He just always seemed to be around.

But maybe I was wrong. Maybe Callum didn't like me like that.

When I started thinking about our game of kissy tag yesterday, I started to think I had made a mistake.

The way Callum had stood on the field, and how hard he had tried to get away—maybe Callum had never wanted to kiss me after all.

CHAPTER SIX

Over the weekend, I didn't see Callum or Alex. But by Monday morning, I was feeling better. News travels fast at my school. But it turns into old news pretty fast, too.

When I got to school, Alex wasn't there yet.

I did a slow walk around—that kind of walk where you check things out, but pretend you're totally relaxed. Secretly,

I wanted to see if Callum was back at school yet.

Once Callum came back, I wanted things to go back to normal—just us goofing around, like we always did.

I didn't like Callum or his friends being angry with me. I just wanted our game of kissy tag to disappear like a bad dream.

As I passed a group of little kids, they all stopped talking and looked at me. But they stayed quiet.

I pretended not to notice. But as I walked around the corner, I half looked back at them, trying to hear if they were going to say anything.

Big mistake.

"Hey! Watch where you're going!"

Mickey was standing right there. Two inches from my face. I was so close I could have kissed him. I had been so busy looking back at the little kids that I hadn't seen where I was going.

Mickey jumped back and brushed himself off like I had fleas.

"Oh, sorry," I mumbled.

But I wasn't looking at Mickey.

Callum was sitting on his bag with his arm in a bright blue sling.

I just stood there, looking at him. His eyes looked nice against his sling. But things had gotten off to a bad start.

"So," I said, trying to sound like I was cool, but I felt weird. "How's your arm?" I asked Callum.

"My arm's fine," Callum said. "But my collarbone hurts like anything."

His friends laughed.

My cheeks started to burn. Now I had no idea what to do. Callum was looking at me like he was waiting for me to go away.

So that's what I did.

I walked off, feeling really bad. Now I was sure that I had it all wrong. Callum didn't like me. At least, not in a kissing kind of way.

But that didn't matter now. It didn't even seem like we were friends anymore. Somehow, playing kissy tag had wrecked everything.

Alex didn't make it to school until the bell rang. That's pretty normal for Alex.

So, of course, there was lots to talk

about as we sat down for class. I couldn't start the day without first talking to Alex. Not when there was the weekend and boys to discuss.

I was right in the middle of telling Alex about what Callum had said that morning, when I heard a strange voice yelling:

"Everyone listen up, please!"

I stopped talking to Alex and sat up straight.

There, standing in front of our class, was a substitute teacher. She was really tall and had a big jaw like a man.

But that wasn't the worst of it.

The worst part was what she was saying. "I'll be teaching you for the next few weeks," she said in a booming voice.

Few weeks! Suddenly, Callum and kissy tag weren't my only problems. Mrs. Tran was my favorite teacher ever.

The substitute teacher kept talking about all the work she was going to give us. But I couldn't concentrate.

Where's Mrs. Tran?

What was wrong with Mrs. Tran? It wasn't like her to leave us with a mean teacher. Was she sick? Had the boys finally given her a nervous breakdown?

I had to know what was going on.

"What's wrong with Mrs. Tran?" I called out.

The substitute teacher frowned. She looked even meaner when she did that. "No calling out in class," she said.

Right away, I put up my hand. We were allowed to ask questions, weren't we?

But the substitute teacher frowned even more. "You're Rebecca Olsen, aren't you?" she said.

I nodded, feeling worried.

Normally, I wouldn't mind if a new teacher knew my name. You never know what people have been saying.

It could be something really good like, *There's Becky Olsen. She's going to be a famous artist one day.*

Or maybe, *There's Becky Olsen. She's the kindest, smartest, prettiest girl in the school.*

Well, a girl can dream!

But after the events of the past few days, I had a feeling that it would be more like, *There's Becky Olsen. She broke a boy's collarbone playing kissy tag. And what's worse—he doesn't even like her like that!*

In the end, the substitute teacher didn't answer my question. She just kept talking about how she was going to "do things" and what she "expected from us."

So now I was stuck in a class with a bunch of boys *and* a teacher who hated me. And all because of playing kissy tag.

CHAPTER
SEVEN

"Yay! Thanks, Mom!"

Alex and I ran, cheering and clapping down the hall into my room.

"That's five *altogether*," Mom called out after us.

"Thanks, Mom!" I called out again, before I shut my bedroom door.

Finally, something good was happening to me. Mom was letting me have my birthday party at the movies. But even better, we were allowed to watch the movie without any adults.

"So, who are you going to invite?" Alex asked.

She was already sitting at my desk with a piece of paper in front of her. She wrote our names at the top of the list.

I lay down on my bed. "Only three more, huh?"

We were both quiet, thinking.

Three weeks ago, it would have been easy. Alex and me, plus Callum and his friends Mickey and Brad. That made five. Perfect!

I liked the idea of inviting boys to my

party. And three weeks ago, Callum and his friends were part of our group. But we didn't hang around with them anymore. Mickey was still acting like he hates us. And I wasn't talking much to Callum.

"What about Darcy and her friends?" Alex asked.

"Yeah, Darcy's cool," I said.

But I was thinking about Callum.

"Only, there's four in her group," Alex said, scribbling out some names. "That's too many."

We were quiet for a while. I thought about how things used to be, before we played kissy tag. Before the mean substitute teacher arrived.

Alex started drawing flower patterns on the paper.

"What do you think is wrong with Mrs. Tran?" I asked. "She must be pretty sick to be away for this long."

"Dunno," Alex said, still drawing. "Hey, what about the Basketball Girls?"

"Yeah, I like them," I said.

We all call Angie and Claire the Basketball Girls because they always play basketball at lunchtime.

"Except that's only four for the party," Alex said.

"That's OK," I said. "We'll still have fun."

But I didn't feel as excited anymore. My birthday list didn't feel quite right.

After Alex went home, I kept thinking about Mrs. Tran, and Callum.

I used to look forward to going to school. Mrs. Tran is a great teacher. And Callum is my second-best friend.

At least he *used* to be.

I pulled out a fresh piece of paper and started drawing a border around the edge. It took forever. There were a lot of tiny leaves and flowers to color in. When I'd finished, the paper had a tangled green vine with red and yellow flowers all around the edge.

It looked pretty good.

I stared at the blank part in the middle of the paper.

If I wrote a letter to Callum, I wondered, *would he forgive me? Would he be my friend again?*

But I didn't really think anything could make Callum be my friend again.

I added a few more leaves to the border.
Then I started writing in the middle.
Slowly. Carefully. In my very best writing:

Dear Mrs. Tran,
GET WELL SOON!
We miss you.

I did hearts instead of dots. And,
inside the two o's for "soon," I did two
sad faces.

Then I turned the paper over and wrote "Becky Olsen" on the back.

Maybe I couldn't fix things with Callum. But I could write a note to Mrs. Tran.

Even if that doesn't seem like much, it felt good to be doing something.

CHAPTER EIGHT

The next day, class started out as usual—with the substitute teacher yelling.

"Rebecca, quiet please!"

Actually, now that I think about it, class usually started with the substitute teacher yelling *at me*.

Sometimes, it was because I was talking.

And last week, I spoke back to her about my pen privilege.

Now that Callum could hardly write, I was the only one in our class allowed to write with a pen. I had worked really hard to earn that pen privilege with Mrs. Tran.

But the substitute teacher had said that she didn't do things like that. She said that I would have to use a pencil until *everyone* in the class was ready to move on to pens.

I'll never be able to use a pen, then!

Judging from the messy boys' writing, that would mean waiting until high school!

But today was definitely one morning when I didn't want the substitute teacher yelling at me.

I had been quietly passing around my card for Mrs. Tran so that everyone could sign it.

Then Darcy had asked me, "What if we don't miss Mrs. Tran? Do we still have to sign our name?"

I just shrugged.

When I got back to my desk, I whispered to Alex, "Glad we crossed Darcy off the party list."

That was when the trouble started.

Darcy was waving the card around like it was a flag.

"Darcy, are you passing around notes?" asked the teacher.

"No, Miss," said Darcy, in a sickly sweet voice. It made me wonder why I ever thought of inviting Darcy to my party.

"Give that to me, please."

And before my eyes, the exact thing happened that I definitely didn't want to happen. Darcy passed my card up to the teacher.

We were all quiet while she read it. I could see her looking at my writing— I had done it in pen. Then she turned it over and read all the names.

"Who did this?" she asked.

But the strange thing was, she wasn't angry. She had a sad kind of look on her face.

I put up my hand.

"Very good work, Rebecca," she said.

Then she pulled a big envelope from her desk drawer and put the card inside.

"A few more people need to sign their names," she said, as she put the envelope on my desk. "Once everyone's done that, I'll make sure Mrs. Tran gets the card."

Then the substitute teacher smiled at me. And for a split second, she even stopped looking mean.

By late morning, I had everyone's names on the card, except one. It didn't matter how many times I sent the card around the room, it always came back without Callum's name on it.

I knew Callum could hardly write with his left hand. But that didn't matter. I wanted everyone to sign the card—that was the whole point.

When the bell rang for lunch, I slipped over to Callum's desk. He was a bit slow putting away his work with one hand.

Soon, it was just us left in the classroom.

"Best for last!" I said, and put the card on Callum's desk.

But Callum shook his head. "Have you seen how messy my writing is now?" he said.

"That doesn't matter!" I said. "Mrs. Tran won't mind."

He shook his head again. His shoulder still looked stiff.

"Go on," I said gently.

I handed him a pen and held the card down so it wouldn't move around.

Callum sighed. But, slowly, he started to write his name.

It was quiet in the room. I could hear Callum breathing as he worked.

"Not bad!" I said, when he had finished.

"Not bad for a kindergartner!" Callum said, and laughed.

I laughed, too.

"It's your birthday soon, isn't it?" said Callum.

I nodded, putting the card back in its envelope. But I could hear my heart beating now.

"Doing anything good?" he asked.

"Um, maybe the movies," I mumbled.

But my mind was racing. Callum had been to all of my birthday parties so far. *Should I invite him to this one after all?*

"Sounds good!" he said, as he walked out to lunch.

I was left alone in the classroom, wondering what was going on.

Was Callum still my friend or not?

CHAPTER
NINE

"I'll give it to him," said Alex, her eyes sparkling just like the day Callum and I were meant to kiss.

I shook my head and held on tight to the invitation in my hand.

"But he'd be the only boy," I said.

Alex shrugged. "That doesn't matter."

It was lunchtime, and only two days before my birthday party.

The invitation wasn't for Alex or the Basketball Girls—they had already said they could come.

In my hand was a birthday invitation for Callum. Inside, around all the details about the party, I had written,

Birthday Party

❀

Dear Callum,
I'm sorry about your collarbone.
If you're still angry, that's OK.
You don't have to come.

❀

But now I felt nervous about giving it to him. I didn't even know if Callum was my friend anymore.

"Come on, Bec," Alex said, her hands on her hips. "Just give it to him."

"Nah," I said. I thought about how angry Callum had been. "He won't want to come anyway."

I started to put the invitation in my pocket. But Alex snatched it away from me.

"Well, if you won't give it to him, I will," she said.

She started to walk away with the invitation. At first, I didn't know what to do. I just stood there with my mouth open.

But then I started to feel angry.

This was *my* party. And Callum used to be *my* friend.

This had nothing to do with Alex. *Maybe if she hadn't started talking about kissing in the first place, then Callum and I would still be friends. Why did I always let Alex take over?*

I felt anger surging through me, and started to run.

I caught up with Alex in a flash and

This has nothing to do with Alex! It's MY party!

snatched the invitation back before she knew what was happening.

"It's my party, Alex!" I yelled.

Alex stopped and stared at me.

Right away I felt bad for yelling. "Callum's *my* friend," I said quietly.

"Oh," Alex said, and looked at her feet.

"I'll give it to him myself," I said, and tried to smile.

"OK," Alex said.

But I kept standing there, feeling bad.

Then Alex started to smile. "Well, hurry up then!" she said. "I'll meet you at the steps."

Alex winked and then headed the other way. That's one of my favorite things about Alex—she doesn't hold a grudge.

I gulped and started looking around for Callum. Now I *had* to give him the invitation.

"Becky, wait!"

Callum was running after me.

I had just given him the invitation, but I didn't hang around to watch him open it.

"I'm not angry," Callum said, when he had caught up with me.

"That's good," I said, quietly, looking at Callum's shoes. His feet are really big these days.

"Yeah, I realized that you didn't trip me," Callum said, smiling.

"Really?"

Now I forgot to feel shy. This was something new.

"If you tripped me, that would mean you caught me," Callum said, laughing. "And there's no way you did that!"

"Oh, really?" I said, looking up at him.

But I was laughing, too. Now it didn't seem to matter what had really happened.

After that, we really talked for the first time since we played kissy tag. Not about anything big, but it still felt great.

"So, are we still friends?" I said after a while.

We're still friends!

"Sure," Callum said, his eyes shining. He tucked the invitation into his sling and held out his left hand for me to shake.

For a moment, I wasn't sure what to do. It's not like I go around shaking people's hands every day.

Then I slipped my hand into his and we shook.

I wasn't looking at Callum's face, but his hand felt nice and strong in my hand.

"Friends," Callum said, and walked away.

I headed for Alex and the steps.

I couldn't stop grinning. It felt great to be friends with Callum again. And there was something about that handshake that made me feel amazing.

CHAPTER TEN

I couldn't help feeling sorry for poor Callum. He must have really missed playing basketball because of his collarbone.

I had been worried that he wouldn't have anyone to talk to at my movie party—him being the only boy.

But as it turned out, Callum did more talking than anyone.

He kept asking Angie and Claire about

their basketball team, and whether their coach was any good.

The three of them stood, huddled together in the theater lobby, talking about dribbling and drills and shots at the basket.

They kept moving their bodies like they were really playing and taking shots in the air with pretend balls.

Callum looked like he was itching to really play.

After a while, Alex raised her eyebrows and looked at me as if to say, *What's going on here?*

I just shrugged. I was pleased Callum was getting along well with the Basketball Girls, but I started to wonder whether

Callum really liked Angie or Claire. I mean, in a kissing kind of way.

Maybe that was why he hadn't wanted to kiss me, I suddenly thought. *Because he really liked one of them!*

Maybe he really likes Angie or Claire?

So I just stood there, at my own party, wondering how I would feel if Callum kissed someone else.

It wasn't exactly my favorite part of

the day. But then I decided that I really didn't mind. I had nearly lost Callum as a friend because of kissy tag. All that kissing stuff had been a lot more trouble than it was worth.

If Callum wanted to kiss someone else, then that was fine with me. Just as long as he was still my friend, I didn't care what he did.

After a while, Callum looked over at me and said, "Becky, you should play basketball."

I shook my head, but I was smiling. "I'm too short," I said.

Callum grinned. "You're fast enough, though!" he said.

We all laughed.

By the time we went in for the movie, I was feeling good. I had all my favorite friends with me on my birthday. No more problems because of kissy tag, and no adults around.

What more could a girl ask for?

Everyone else was having fun, too.

Alex started telling gross jokes to Angie and Claire.

They were all laughing really loud as they sat down together. So it turned out that they sat next to each other, then me, then Callum on the end.

"Do you want to sit next to someone else?" I asked Callum. If he liked Angie or Claire, then he wouldn't want to be stuck with me.

"You're the birthday girl, aren't you?" Callum said.

Then the lights dimmed and the previews started on the screen.

"Besides," he said softly, "you're the first girl I've held hands with."

I looked at him in the dark. I wasn't sure if I had heard him right.

"What do you mean?" I asked.

I had to lean in so he could hear me above the noise of the previews.

"When we shook hands the other day at school," came back Callum's voice in the dark. "That's almost the same as holding hands."

Then, in the dim light, I could see Callum holding out his good hand. It was palm up, like he wanted to hold my hand.

By now, my heart was pounding even louder than the noise from the screen.

At least, that was how it felt.

I glanced over at Alex and the others. But they were laughing about one of the previews. They still weren't doing a very good job of keeping quiet.

Slowly, I reached out and slipped my hand into Callum's. We rested our hands on the armrest between us.

His hand felt warm, like he was holding me in a hug. It felt wonderful.

A couple of times during the movie, Alex shook her bag of popcorn at Callum and me. But she didn't realize that we were holding hands.

Holding hands in the dark like that felt like the biggest, best secret.

When the movie finished, we stopped holding hands, but we still seemed joined somehow.

As we walked out into the lobby, Callum smiled at me and I smiled back.

"Why are you smiling?" asked Alex.

I just shrugged. "I'm happy!" I said.

I wasn't going to tell Alex what had happened. Not for a while at least—it had nothing to do with her.

It was something special and secret, between Callum and me.

This time we didn't have Alex counting us down for a kiss, or the adults laughing, or the whole school whispering about us. This was none of their business.

Callum is the first boy I ever held hands with. I'm going to remember how that feels for the rest of my life.

THE END

She loves her first modern dance
class, but now she's worried
about the performance!

Keep reading for an excerpt.

CHAPTER ONE

~ Rosie's ~
DANCE ACADEMY

Charlie looked up at the sign and grinned. Here she was at last—at a real dance school. No more dancing in the cold church basement. No more boring ballet classes with old Miss Plum.

Charlie was finally at a real school that taught modern dance.

She hitched her bag higher on her shoulder, took a deep breath, and pushed on the heavy old door.

She could already hear music pounding from the studio above. From the thudding and clapping, it sounded like a toddler class. Or maybe junior beginners.

For months, Charlie had begged her parents to let her start dancing here. At first, they had just said no. The classes cost a lot of money. And to get here, Charlie had to catch a bus all by herself.

But two weeks ago, as a birthday surprise, Charlie's parents had said yes.

Quietly, Charlie climbed up the stairs. Soon, she came to another door and another sign.

Charlie smiled to herself. Yet another thing that was different from her old ballet classes! This dance school was the real thing.

She was still smiling as she pushed open the second door.

But as she walked in and scanned the waiting area, Charlie gulped away her smile and felt her heart pounding quickly in her chest. Suddenly, the dance school seemed a long way from home.

It's her first PJ party! But what if something embarrassing happens?

GO GIRL!

sleep-over!

BY ROWAN McAULEY

Keep reading for an excerpt!

CHAPTER
*ONE

It was six o'clock on Friday morning, the last day of school for the year. The alarm hadn't gone off yet, but Olivia was already awake, dressed, and sitting at the kitchen table, eating her toast and waiting for her mom to get up.

She drank a glass of milk and ate an apple, but her mom still slept on. She brushed her teeth and made her lunch, but even then her mom did not stir.

Olivia checked the clock on the microwave. Six thirty. Surely her mom should be awake by now? She tiptoed along the hallway and looked in. Her mom was fast asleep, snoring slightly. Olivia knocked gently on the open door. Her mom did not move.

Olivia cleared her throat, "Ahem!"

Her mom rolled over in bed and snored more loudly. Olivia was getting desperate.

"Mom," she whispered.

"Mom," she said gently.

"Mom!" she said more firmly.

This was getting her nowhere.

"MOM!" she yelled suddenly and stamped her foot.

"Hmm?" said her mom, sitting up in bed, her hair all fluffy on one side. "What's up, baby?"

"Mom," said Olivia. "You have to get up. I am sleeping over at Ching Ching's house tonight."

"Are you?" said her mom. "Are you sure? Did we talk about this?"

"Mom," said Olivia sternly, because she had to be strict with her mom sometimes. "You know it is. We talked about it on Monday, remember? You spoke with Mrs. Adams on the phone."

"I know, baby," said her mom,

yawning. "I'm just teasing you."

"Well," said Olivia, "will you get up now?"

"Mmm," said her mom, still sounding tired. "What time is it?"

"Six thirty," said Olivia. "Or even later by now. We've been talking for at least five minutes."

"Six thirty?"

"Or six thirty-five," said Olivia.

"Is the sun even up yet?" asked her mom.

"Mom!"

"OK, OK," said her mom. "I'm getting up. Even though it's still the middle of the night," she grumbled.

"Come on," said Olivia. "Here's your bathrobe."

While her mom took a shower, Olivia checked her bag again. As well as her lunchbox, she had packed her pajamas, her swimsuit, some clean clothes for tomorrow, her hairbrush, and a small box of chocolates for Ching Ching's mom, to say thank you. Was that everything?

It was almost seven o'clock and Olivia was dancing with impatience, waiting for her mom to finish blow-drying her hair. Finally, she was ready.

"OK," she said to Olivia. "Now, are you sure you have packed everything you need?"

"Yes," said Olivia.

"Pajamas?"

"Yes," said Olivia.

"Chocolates for Mrs. Adams?"

"Yes," said Olivia.

"Clean underwear for tomorrow?"

"Mom!"

"Well, have you?"

"YES!" said Olivia. "Come on!"

"All right!" said her mom. "Just checking.

I'll just get the keys. . . . "

But Olivia was already out the door and waiting at the front gate, her backpack on her back. Her mom locked the door and walked down the path (so slowly!), and together they walked to the bus stop.

"I'm going to miss you tonight," said her mom.

"Yeah, yeah," said Olivia, looking ahead for the bus.

"I will. I won't see you all day, I won't have anyone to eat dinner with, and you'll be at Ching Ching's until tomorrow. . . ."

"I know," said Olivia.

"What time am I picking you up?"

"Lunchtime," said Olivia. "Ching Ching

and I will have breakfast together, and play in the morning, and then you can pick me up at lunchtime."

"Lunchtime it is," said her mom, giving her a hug and a big smoochy kiss.

The bus was just arriving at the corner.

"Bye, mom," said Olivia, yelling back over her shoulder as she ran to catch it.

At last she was on her way.

�֍

If you loved
this story, don't
miss the rest of
the series!